STO

Robin

FRIENDS
OF ACPL

W9-CMT-841

Chickadee

Northern Flicker

Ruffed Grouse

Cedar Waxwing

Crow

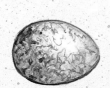
Rose-Breasted
Grosbeak

Moose

Bluebird

Loon

Northern Shrike

Red-Winged Blackbird

Moose Eggs

Or, Why Moose Have Flat Antlers

Story copyright © 2007 by Susan Williams Beckhorn.
Illustrations © 2007 by Helen Stevens. All rights reserved.
Typography by the Roxmont Group
Printed in China

FCI   5   4   3   2   1

LIBRARY OF CONGRESS CATALOGING-IN-PUBLICATION DATA

Beckhorn, Susan Williams, 1953–
    Moose eggs or, why moose have flat antlers / by Susan Williams
Beckhorn ; [illustrations by Helen Stevens].
        p.   cm.
    Summary: Mrs. Moose and Mrs. Grouse watch humorously as
their bumbling but well-intentioned husbands try to find and
incubate "moose eggs," in this story that explains why moose have
broad, flat antlers, a droopy nose, and wide hooves.
    ISBN 978-0-89272-689-9 (hardcover : alk. paper)
    [1. Moose--Fiction. 2. Animals--Infancy--Fiction. 3. Grouse--Fiction.
4. Humorous stories.] I. Stevens, Helen, ill. II. Title.
    PZ7.B381735Mo 2007
    [E]--dc22
                                        2007006471

Down East Books
A division of Down East Enterprise, Inc.
Publisher of Down East, the Magazine of Maine

Book orders: 1-800-685-7962 / www.downeastbooks.com
Distributed to the trade by National Book Network

Moose Eggs

Or, Why Moose Have Flat Antlers

By Susan Williams Beckhorn
Illustrated by Helen Stevens

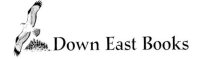 Down East Books

In the morning of the
world, Moose was not the splay-footed,
hump-backed, shovel-antlered creature that we know today.
He looked much like his cousin Deer did before Deer got his long, wagging,
white tail—but that is another story. There are many such stories! Raccoon
did not always have a black mask and a ringed tail. Porcupine did not

always have prickles. And
little, striped Skunk was once glossy
black all over and did not smell a bit. The Maker of
the World loves making and changing things. But sometimes we change
ourselves, and that is what happened to the Father of all Moose—all because
he wanted something very special.

What Moose wanted was a baby moose. But Moose's wife said, "Babies come all in good time."

Moose didn't like to wait. He went to talk to his friend, Grouse.

He found Grouse in a clearing, scratching for bugs. Grouse and his wife had eight pretty little puff balls, which were baby grouse, pecking about their feet.

Moose told Grouse about his problem. "How did you get *your* babies?" he asked.

Grouse puffed up his feathers importantly. "Oh, that was simple. Mrs. Grouse sat on a nest one day, and when she got up, there was a nice little egg under her. That kept happening until she had eight of them. Then, one day, out popped all these babies!"

One of the chicks pecked Grouse's toe. "Ouch!" he said.

"But I don't have a nest," said Moose.

Grouse looked at his big friend's antlers. They were not the broad, flat antlers that Moose wears on his head today. They were slim, with many branches, like a tree. They almost looked as if they were meant to hold something.

"Yes you do." said Grouse. "Your antlers would make a great nest."

"But how will I get some moose eggs to put in my nest?" asked Moose.

Grouse thought for a while, then said, "That's easy. There are lots of eggs

down by the trout stream. The big gray ones must be moose eggs. I don't know whose the other, smaller ones are."

Moose ran right to the trout stream and searched until he found several big, round, smooth moose eggs. He nodded to himself, thinking, *They look big and strong, just like moose babies should look.*

But when he tried to pick up the moose eggs, he found they were *very* heavy. He pushed and rolled them, but he could only lift two with his antlers. He staggered a little under their weight, but he was happy. Soon, when these eggs hatched, he would have two big, fine baby moose!

Moose's wife tried not to laugh when she saw Moose staggering along with the two great moose eggs cradled carefully in his antlers. "I don't think that's how you get baby moose," she said to her husband.

"Yes it is. Grouse told me so," said Moose. "And he knows about hatching babies. He and Mrs. Grouse have eight of them!"

Now Moose had another question for Grouse: "How long does it take for eggs to hatch?" he panted.

Grouse had no idea how long it took for moose eggs to hatch, but he knew exactly how long it took for grouse eggs to hatch. "Twenty-one to twenty-eight days," he answered, fluffing his ruff importantly.

"Whew," said Moose. "I don't know if I can carry these eggs in my nest that long."

"They won't hatch if they fall out of the nest," warned Grouse.

So, day after day, Moose carried his eggs.

He carried them up mountains

and down mountains.

He carried them over meadows and through marshes.

He carried them through pine woods and birch woods.

Often he had to rest his chin on the ground because the eggs were so heavy.

Twenty-one days passed. Nothing happened.

Seven more days passed,
and still nothing happened.

"Why don't my eggs hatch?" asked Moose.

Grouse didn't know why Moose's eggs had not hatched, but he didn't want to say so. "Go ask your wife," he said. "Maybe moose eggs take longer than grouse eggs."

"When do you think moose eggs hatch?" Moose asked his wife.

Moose's wife scratched her head on the rough bark of a maple tree while she thought about his question.

Finally she said, "Probably it is too late in the summer now. I think it would be a good idea if our baby moose were to hatch early in the spring, when the ice melts and there are tender water lily shoots to eat—just about the same time that grouse babies hatch."

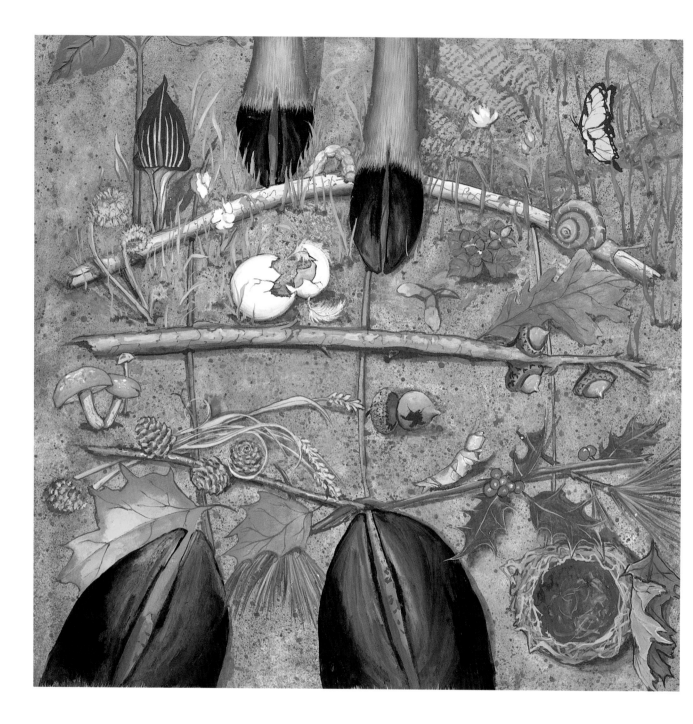

Moose counted on his feet almost three times. As he did so, he noticed that they looked bigger than they used to.

"Next spring won't happen for another eleven months! Eleven months is a very long time to carry these eggs in my nest," he said.

"Well, you have already carried them for one month," his wife pointed out.

Just then, Grouse came hurrying up. "I forgot something!" he said. "Once you have eggs in the nest, someone has to sit on them."

"Why?" asked Moose.

"I don't know. You just do—or at least my wife always does," said Grouse. "I'm sorry I forgot to tell you this before." Ducking his head to avoid looking his friend in the eye, Grouse noticed a sun-warmed spot of sandy earth nearby and decided that this was a good time to go take a dust bath.

Moose looked at his wife. "Will you sit on our eggs?" he asked.

Moose's wife stared at him. "No, I will not," she said. "It wouldn't be very comfy, and I have better things to do for the next eleven months. Besides, I might crush you."

Moose almost cried.

"I will sit on your eggs," said Grouse. "I don't have anything better to do."

So Moose carried his eggs and Grouse sat on them. Grouse didn't weigh very much, which was good.

But gradually Moose's shoulders grew humped from the weight of the two great moose eggs. His feet became even wider and larger.

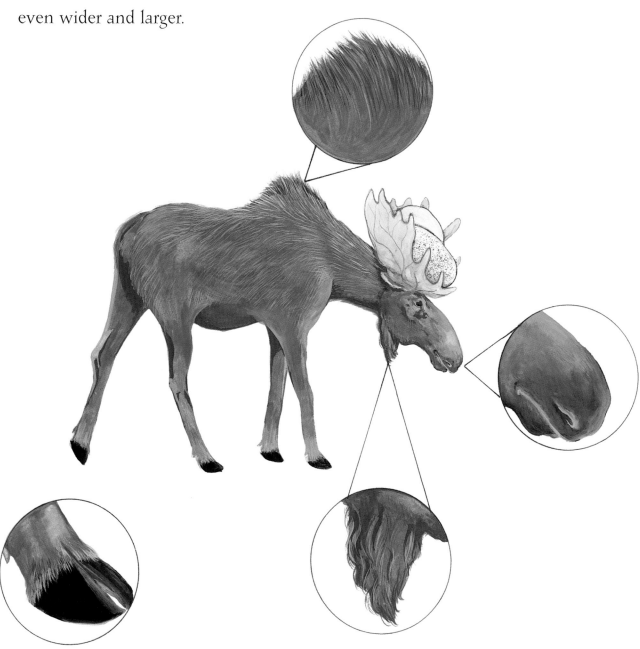

His nose became droopy because he kept resting it on the ground when he got tired. He grew a sort of beard from dragging his chin through the bushes.

And his antlers grew wide and flat from carrying those eggs!

Then, in the middle of winter, something terrible happened.

One day, when he was rubbing them against a tree, Moose's antlers fell off!
The moose eggs tumbled into the snow and rolled right down the hill, back
to the trout stream.

Moose couldn't help it. He cried.

Moose's wife tried to comfort him. "Maybe that wasn't the way to get babies after all," she said.

Grouse said, "I think those eggs were duds. It happens sometimes. When you grow new antlers next spring, we'll try again."

"Thanks," said Moose. "I will do that."

It was a very long wait until springtime when Moose's antlers grew again, and this time, right from the start, they grew out broad and flat instead of narrow and pointy.

"This spring, I'll sit on the eggs from the very beginning," said Grouse.

"And I won't rub against any trees," said Moose.

As soon as the new antlers were big enough, Moose and Grouse hurried to the trout stream and found two nice new eggs.

Then they went to show them to Moose's wife. When they found her, she was up to her knees in a pond, eating lily pads. Before Moose could open his mouth, she said, "I have a surprise for you!"

She mooed softly, and out from behind a balsam fir at the edge of the bog stepped two fuzzy, knobby-kneed, very foolish looking baby moose!

"These are your children, Sphagnum and Hemlock," she told him proudly.

Moose was so astonished that he dropped his two new eggs—*Splash! Splash!* Grouse squawked and flapped quickly away.

"Guess what?" said Moose's wife. "Baby moose don't hatch out of moose eggs after all."

Moose felt lightheaded. He studied the moose eggs, which now lay in the shallow water at the edge of the pond, to make sure that the moose calves had not come out of them. The eggs were just as smooth and round as ever.

He looked at his children and smiled. They did not look foolish to him. They looked big and handsome and strong—just exactly as baby moose should look.

Moose's wife liked his new antlers. "The babies both have humps and noses and big feet like you. Maybe Sphagnum will have flat antlers when he grows up, just like his daddy," she said.

Moose looked at his reflection in the bog. His new antlers still looked like

a perfect nest for carrying eggs, but he was very relieved to know that baby moose do NOT hatch out of moose eggs! Then he remembered all those months he'd spent carrying two great, heavy boulders on his antlers.

"I think I'll go have a little talk with Grouse," he said.

The End

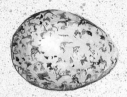
Blue Jay

Cardinal

Phoebe

Goldfinch

Baltimore Oriole

Cormorant

Osprey

Ruby-Throated
Hummingbird

Mallard

White-Breasted
Nuthatch

Puffin

Catbird